THE MAN WHO CHANGED ROOMS

THE MAN WHO CHANGED ROOMS

JOHNSTON McCULLEY

WILDSIDE PRESS

THE MAN WHO CHANGED ROOMS

Originally published in *Clues* magazine,
February 2, 1929.

THE MAN WHO
CHANGED ROOMS

CHAPTER I

INSTRUCTIONS

Because he was not absolutely sure that the tall, hawk-nosed man was shadowing him and watching every move that he made, Creighton Marpe was compelled to stifle his feelings and resort to strategy rather than violence.

He had an inclination to turn abruptly and drive his fist squarely to the end of the hawk nose, and he was thoroughly capable of doing it. But he had to be sure. It would not do to make a mistake. It certainly would not look well for a man in Creighton Marpe's position to smash an innocent pedestrian on the nose.

Creighton Marpe was compelled to remember that he was in a most particular branch of government service, and that the enemies of the Government were his enemies. They were sly, crafty, even violent on occasion. It might serve their purposes to lead him into a nasty row.

So Creighton Marpe merely continued down the Avenue after the manner of a gentleman leisurely taking the air and enjoying the splendid afternoon, swinging his stick as though he did not have a care or suspicion in the world; and the expression on his face was as guileless as that of an innocent babe.

He stopped now and then and pretended to be peering in at shop windows and scrutinizing the latest wares, and once to touch flaming match to tip of cigarette. On these occasions he made certain that the man with the hawk nose was still in the vicinity. The latter certainly acted as though he was making it his business to keep Creighton Marpe in sight.

There must be some sort of big game coming off," Marpe muttered, as he dodged the traffic in a cross street. "And the others evidently know more about it than I. Matter of fact, I do not know anything — yet."

He was on his way now to a rendezvous with his chief, who had arrived only that morning from Washington. The manner of rendezvous told Marpe that something was afoot. For he had been instructed by telephone to cancel previous arrangements and meet the Chief in a certain place near Washington Square, and to be very careful about it.

Creighton Marpe was rather an impressive-looking gentleman as he continued slowly through the crowd of afternoon shoppers that congested the walk on the fashionable Avenue. He was slightly more than thirty, tall, handsome, and fastidiously dressed. There was nothing of the fop about him, however. He had the appearance of an athlete, and bore an air of command.

Now he made his way through the crowd until he came to a big tobacco shop on a busy corner, moving slowly so that the man behind could keep in sight if he desired to do so. The tobacco shop itself presented a busy scene, with shoppers three deep in front of the counters, salesmen jumping about, men struggling to get to the cigar lighters and telephone booths.

Creighton Marpe sought a telephone booth and was fortunate to find one unoccupied. He entered it and closed the sound-proof glass door behind him. He went through all the motions of putting in a telephone call — dropping a coin into the slot, moving his lips as though in denunciation of an inefficient "central," then smiling like a man who finally has been given the correct number and is speaking to somebody with whom it pleases him to converse.

And all the time he was doing these things he was holding down the receiver-hook with his elbow. His acting was for the benefit of anybody who might be watching him. His subterfuge was for the purpose of learning whether the hawk-nosed man really was trailing him.

The hawk-nosed man entered the tobacco shop and made his way through the crowd. He glanced through the door of the telephone booth, and Creighton Marpe was quite sure that he saw the other's eyelids flutter betrayingly as their glances met. So! He was being followed, trailed, watched, shadowed like a criminal by the hawk-nosed man!

It was all in the game. Yet Creighton Marpe felt like rushing from the telephone booth and calling the other to account. But he probably would be confronted by an air of injured innocence if he did, and be termed a meddling fool, he decided. Also, by doing such a thing he would attract attention to himself at a time when he did not wish to do so; and he might even be walking straight into a trap prepared for him. The part of wisdom, all things considered, was to ignore the other man — and dodge him.

So Creighton Marpe stepped from the telephone booth with a whimsical smile upon his lips, aping the expression of a man who probably had just concluded a satisfactory conversation over the wire with a lady.

He thrust his way forward to the counter and purchases a package of cigarettes that he did not need. But it gave him an opportunity to look over those in the shop. The hawk-nosed man, he found, was standing in the rear, near the door that opened into the side street.

Creighton Marpe started toward the front door of the shop in a natural manner. As he reached it, he saw the hawk-nosed man dark out the rear door with the evident intention of circling the corner and taking to the trail again. But Creighton Marpe immediately turned and made his way back through the shop, and went out the rear door behind the other. He started down the cross street and walked briskly.

"Hope that he runs in circles until he's dizzy!" Marpe muttered to himself.

When he reached the first corner, Creighton Marpe swung to the left again, used the parallel street for several blocks, and then returned to the Avenue. Here the walks were not so badly crowded. Marpe did not see the hawk-nosed man. He stepped along briskly now, thinking of keeping the appointment with his Chief, wondering what it was that had caused his superior to arrange a meeting in this section of the city.

He crossed the Square, turned into a side street, and passed the small apartment house which was to be the rendezvous. At the next corner he crossed the street and returned on the opposite side. So far as he could see, he was not under surveillance.

Now he went across the street again and into the building, where a girl sat behind a combined desk and switchboard.

"Ring Mr. Daggern, please," Creighton Marpe said, as he had been instructed. "Mr. Howland calling."

The girl surveyed him languidly and smiled. Creighton Marpe had a way of getting a welcoming smile from women. A moment later she assured him that he was to go right up, and that the room number was 316.

"Come in!" a man's voice commanded.

Creighton Marpe did not recognize the voice. It certainly was not that of his Chief. So he turned the knob of the door, threw the door open, and stepped swiftly to one side of it instead of into the room.

Nothing happened. Marpe then peered around the

corner of the casement. The Chief was standing a few feet away, grinning.

"All right!" the Chief called. "Glad to see that you are so wary. Come right in, please."

Marpe closed the door and turned to face them again. The Chief beckoned and led the way into a little adjoining room. He introduced the other man as Captain Gaines, and the captain immediately went back into the front room and closed the connecting door.

"Sit down, Marpe," the Chief said, kindly, waving a hand toward a chair. "All this is rather mystifying to you, no doubt. Quite like intrigue, isn't it? Captain Gaines is working with the General Staff, and is with me as a sort of bodyguard."

"Bodyguard, sir?" Marpe asked, his eyebrows raised in surprise.

"Exactly! We are playing with dynamite, or something that is stronger. The enemy is very active. I really do not know all about it myself. But we are rather secretive about this thing. That is why I asked you to come here to get your instructions."

"Then there is work for me to do?" Marpe asked.

"Exactly. You are to go at once, and as speedily as possible, to Kansas City, Missouri. There you will engage a room in the Hotel Baltimore. Captain Makker, an army officer stationed at Fort Leavenworth, will make himself known to you and deliver to you a certain paper."

"I understand, sir," Marpe said.

"You will register at the hotel under your own name, and Captain Makker will be watching and communicate with you immediately. As soon as you have that paper, Marpe, you will bring it with all haste back to New York City."

"Understood, sir," Marpe said, as his superior stopped and looked at him questioningly.

"Upon your return you will engage a room at the

Hotel Magnificent here. A Major Sinlon will make himself known to you, and you will deliver the paper to him. That is all, except that you must make all speed possible."

"It does not sound difficult, sir."

"Ah! I have neglected to inform you that certain persons will do everything to get their hands on that document. My boy, I do not even know what that document is. But I know that the War Department had asked us to do this work, that their own officers are being watched, that they are — well, are really afraid — that the document will fall into the wrong hands. They especially requested that you be given this work to do. You have a wonderful record, Marpe."

"I am grateful, sir."

"I asked them why they didn't have this Captain Makker simply bring the papers on and deliver them to Major Sinlon. From the answer I received, I am led to the conclusion that there is something terrific back of this."

"But couldn't the stuff be memorized by a trustworthy officer, and couldn't he come here or go to Washington and make out the document there?"

"My own question, boy. I was told to mind my own business, in nice, polite words."

"Couldn't a couple of officers come with the paper, one remaining awake and alert all the time?"

"My own question again. Then it was rather intimated to me that perhaps our service couldn't deliver the goods. I replied that our branch of the secret service could do anything from running errands to fighting a war. Matter of pride with us, now, Marpe."

"It doesn't sound like a difficult assignment," Marpe declared.

"Um! It doesn't at that. But it was hinted to me that the enemy, whoever they are, might go to any length to get that document, whatever it is. Confound it, they shouldn't make us work entirely in the dark!"

"My own initiative, sir?" Marpe asked.

"Just do the work, Marpe."

"Very well, Chief. I'll get a plane and —"

"Sorry! I know that you love to ride around the sky, Marpe, but the airplane stuff will not do this trip. Was told as much. It seems they fear the foe will be watching for an airplane. We have specific orders to use the good old railroads."

"Very well, sir; only it will be slower."

"Fast enough to suit them, I suppose."

"Can you tell me anything else, sir?" Marpe asked.

"Very little, I am afraid. They didn't tell me much more than I have told you. Just get to Kansas City, get that document from the Fort Leavenworth officer, come back with it, and deliver it to Major Sinlon at the Hotel Magnificent."

"I was shadowed as I came here today, sir."

"Um! No doubt! I presume they are shadowing every know man to see which gets the assignment."

"He was a tall, hawk-nosed man —"

"So? That gentleman's name is Lenserg. I have heard a few things concerning him, and he is what might be termed a bad customer. Lenserg, huh? Um! This may be more serious than I thought."

"Foreign government, sir?"

"Exactly! European government, the one we of the Service know as Number Six. I have to laugh sometimes, very quietly in the seclusion of my private study. With all these peace pacts and all this disarmament talk, a man would think that there was no sense in having a secret service and special couriers and all that. But we on the inside — well —"

"Yes, sir!" said Creighton Marpe. "I shall be watching for this Mr. Lenserg. I dodged him coming here."

"Good work," the Chief said. "All set now, Marpe?"

"I understand, sir. Any passwords?"

"Yes. I have to laugh again, very quietly, of course. The password will be given you by Captain Makker in Kansas City, and again by Major Sinlon in New York. It is Spanish."

"My favorite foreign language, sir."

"Uh-huh! Here it is — *Feliz Aventura!*"

"The Happy Adventure," Marpe said.

"Exactly! Isn't that silly?" the Chief asked. "Let us hope that it will be a happy adventure for you, Marpe. I'd hate to lose you, my best man."

"You may be sure, sir, that I'll do my best to return," Marpe replied, laughing.

"That's the boy! Eyes and ears open, now! I do not need to tell you that you are in danger from the moment you leave this room. It appears that our friends from over the sea are very eager to get that document. Oh! Here is a photograph of Captain Makker."

He handed Marpe a photograph, and the latter looked at it for some little time, until it was impressed upon his memory to such an extent that he believed he would know the original instantly.

"Recent?"

"New photograph, front and side views, taken especially for this affair," the Chief responded. "And here is one of Major Sinlon, too."

Creighton Marpe inspected the second photograph well also.

"And the password is *Feliz Aventura*," Marpe said. "Very good, sir. I am to work alone?"

"Captain Gaines will join you in the outer room and stay with you until you take the train."

"But I thought that he was your bodyguard."

"He was, Marpe. But I do not need one now. I have given you my instructions. So you are the quarry now.

Good luck, Marpe!"

The gray-haired Chief extended his hand, and Creighton Marpe clasped it, then stepped back a pace and saluted snappily, and then turned to stalk with measured, military tread across the room toward the door.

"Oh, Marpe!"

"Sir?" Marpe turned.

"Along the way, you may encounter a little lady who bears the name of Alla Stimney. You have met her, I believe?"

Creighton Marpe's face flushed. "Yes, sir," he replied.

"All Stimney has no secrets from me, lad. She is the best woman we have in the Service. You are the best man. It is fitting that — er —"

"Yes, sir!" said Marpe.

"She has told me of your little romance. Congratulations, my boy. But do not forget, Marpe — the Service comes first!"

"Always, sir!"

"If there every comes a time when you must choose, and quickly, between the Service and your sweetheart, you will remember that —"

"That the Service comes first — yes, sir!" Marpe interrupted.

"And I sincerely hope that you never will have to make the choice, boy."

"Do I understand that Miss Stimney is on this assignment also, sir?"

"Tut, tut! You should know better than to ask me questions. You may run across her. That's all, Marpe!"

There was cold dismissal in his tone; the Chief was the Chief once more. Marpe opened the door and stepped out into the other room where Captain Gaines was waiting for him.

"When we leave the building, follow me at a short

distance," Marpe requested. "Observe whether I am followed by anybody else. I'll give you the chance, now and then, to overtake me and whisper if there is anything to communicate. Then I'll repass you, and so on."

They went down together in the elevator, but did not speak. In the lobby below, Creighton Marpe stepped briskly through the door and down the short flight of steps to the street, and Captain Gaines followed him leisurely.

As he reached the street, Marpe gasped, and almost came to an abrupt stop. Just across the thoroughfare, leaning against the front of a building, twirling his mustache and smiling in a supercilious manner, was the tall, hawk-nosed man whose name the Chief had said was Lenserg.

CHAPTER II

THE SIGNAL

Creighton Marpe apparently gave him not the slightest attention. He turned up the street and walked to Washington Square, and across it. Captain Gaines followed a short distance behind, and the man Lenserg shadowed Marpe so faithfully that he did not observe Gaines.

Leaving the Square and starting up the Avenue, Marpe walked at a brisker gait. Lenserg kept the same distance from him. And suddenly Marpe stopped at the curb, extracted a cigarette and lighted it, and over his cupped hands observed that Lenserg continued to advance.

Marpe faced him squarely, surveyed him from head to feet and back again. Lenserg continued his advance, seemingly paying not the slightest attention to the man standing at the curb. He came opposite.

"Hello, Lenserg!" Creighton Marpe said.

Lenserg stopped abruptly, an expression of astonishment in his face.

"I beg your pardon?" he said. "Lenserg is my name. But I do not remember of meeting you, sir."

"Not socially. You scarcely would be in my set," Marpe told him. "But you know my name, I dare say. And, as you see, I know yours. Furthermore I know your game."

"Sir? I fail to understand you," Lenserg said.

"Rats! You followed me down the Avenue a short time ago, and I thought that I had dodged you in that tobacco shop. Shadowing me, are you? I dislike being shadowed, Lenserg."

"The streets are free, are they not?"

"Old stuff!" Marpe commented. "I had expected something better of you. Lenserg, I don't like your face. I feel quite sure that if I see much more of it I'll become enraged. And when I become enraged, I fly off the handle, if you can catch my meaning. You are a husky individual, but I feel quite sure, Lenserg, that I can lick you!"

"Aren't you rather belligerent?" Lenserg asked, smiling.

"At times," Creighton Marpe admitted. "I know the game you are playing. It is your privilege to play it. But I don't like to be followed. Lenserg, I am going to the Hotel Magnificent. I expect to have luncheon there with a friend. After that — who knows? Anything else that you would like to know?"

Lenserg's lip curled. "You are quite clever with your tongue," he said. "Are you as clever in other ways?"

"Possibly."

"And just suppose, Mr. Marpe —"

"So you do know my name!"

"Yes. Suppose that I mix it with you here on this corner? I can say that you attacked me for no reason whatsoever. And what would you say in court?"

"I wouldn't appear in court," Marpe told him. "I'd put up cash bail and forget it. If I really had to disclose my Service, I'd do so without detriment of it. And then what would you say? That you are working for a foreign government and trying to deter officials of the United States?"

"I'd stick to my story and pay a fine for fighting," Lenserg said. "But suppose, in that fight, you were injured so that you had to be taken to a hospital? That little trip of yours would be delayed, would it not?"

"Possibly — if I went to a hospital."

"That light stick which you are carrying, Mr. Marpe, would not avail you much against this heavier one in my hand. One blow against the head, and you certainly would be delayed. I may mention that I know how to fence with a cane."

"And can you also fence with a rapier?" Marpe asked.

"I can, if you'll pardon my seeming lack of modesty in saying so."

"You haven't a rapier with you, by any chance?"

"I have not."

"But I have!" said Creighton Marpe. As he spoke, he twisted the handle of the light cane and a blade flashed in the sun.

Lenserg retreated a step. "A sword cane, eh?" he said.

"It is, and a beauty, too. Though I dare say that I'll not need it," Marpe told him, returning the blade.

Lenserg took a quick step forward. "I could smash you down before you could draw it!" he said, his face livid.

"Easy!" Marpe warned. "Three feet behind you, Mr. Lenserg, is a gentleman with his right hand in coat pocket, and I feel quite sure that he has a pistol in that hand."

"The old trick of trying to get me to look behind, eh, so you can catch me off guard?"

"Oh, I say! I am a man of truth," Marpe declared. "Captain Gaines, kindly step around in front and satisfy the gentleman. I thank you, Captain. There he is, Mr. Lenserg. Is it true that you have a weapon in your hand, Captain?"

Captain Gaines grinned and revealed it.

"You see, Mr. Lenserg?" Marpe asked. "We of the

Service are generally doubly protected. Allow me to suggest that you catch a taxicab now and proceed wherever you wish to go. It is immaterial to us, so long as you rid us of your presence."

Lenserg bowed to him. "You win," he said, "for the present. But it is a long road to Kansas City and back." He turned from them and walked briskly up the Avenue.

"Confound it!" Gaines said. "Why wouldn't we beat him up, or have him arrested, or something like that?"

"This is not a time of war, Captain Gaines," Marpe pointed out. "All this sort of work is done under cover, and those connected with it have no official standing outwardly. We are representatives of our government. Would it look nice if a howl went up that we were abusing the nationals of a friendly power? But these are times, Gaines, when I feel like forgetting the Service and doing what most men would feel like doing. Let's catch a taxi, now."

They flagged a cruising taxicab and headed for the Hotel Magnificent.

"I am going to be rather open about this thing," Marpe said. "I'll engage a room at the Magnificent immediately, and have it held for my return. The enemy will find that out, naturally, and be prepared to greet me when I return. But I may not show up there."

"In that case, Major Sinlon will call up that room, somebody will tell him to come right up, and he'll walk into a mess."

"The major can take care of himself, surely. It is the paper that they want, the mysterious document. The major will not have it. What sort of man is Major Sinlon?"

"Middle aged. Capable," Gaines replied.

"Do you know Captain Makker, the man I am to meet in Kansas City?"

"Met him once. Don't' know anything about him

except that he has a good record."

"It seems to me at times that about half the trouble in the world comes from documents," Marpe offered. "Here I am, possibly running into danger and all that on account of some papers. And I do not even know what they are."

"Neither do I," Captain Gaines assured him. "But from the way they have been acting around the Department in Washington, that document is mighty important."

"And I wonder what Major Sinlon will do with it if I get it to him safely. If the enemy knows the game, they'll be prepared to go after Sinlon, won't they?"

"Don't you worry about that," Captain Gaines replied. "I'll be on the job again as soon as Sinlon gets that document — and possibly some others also. I have orders to wait here in New York for your return. I have a room at the Magnificent now."

"And are you fool enough to use it?"

"Not for sleeping purposes," Captain Gaines replied, chuckling a little. "I go there once a day, with my hand on an automatic when I open the door. But where I sleep is nobody's business."

"You've been around!" Marpe said, smiling.

"Yours is the job I'd like to have. There's some excitement and adventure in it."

"Loss of sleep, poky trains, poor hotels at times, peculiar hours and all that," Marpe assured him.

"But it is a great game!"

"No public acclaim like aviators get."

"But think of the service!"

"That's it, Gaines! We serve, and there is a lot of satisfaction in that, at least."

They reached the Hotel Magnificent and Marpe went directly to the office of the manager, to whom he was known personally. He booked a room, explaining that it was to be held ready for him. The manager knew Marpe's work, and promised secrecy.

"But that is not what I want this time," Marpe protested. "Just pretend to keep it quiet, but let it leak out. I want to register regularly, and I don't care who learns what room has been assigned to me."

"Then I'll have the house detectives keep their eyes on the room," the manager offered.

"No, you don't! Give my enemies a chance to work, if they wish to do anything. I have my own plans. 'The Man Who Changed Rooms,' crooks called me in connection with a certain case I was working on. Well, I still live up to the name. I may change to another room as far as actually living in it goes, but I have my own reasons for being registered in this one."

"Anything that you say, Mr. Marpe."

Marpe and Captain Gaines went in to luncheon, then. They got a table in a corner, where they could sit side by side with their backs to a wall, and ordered lavishly. Their quick eyes took in the crowd of diners, but they saw nobody who looked at all suspicious, or who appeared to be giving them special attention.

Marpe started to say something, but stopped speaking abruptly, and Captain Gaines glanced up, on the alert. He beheld a radiant smile on Creighton Marpe's face, and he followed Marpe's gaze and saw a man and woman sitting down at a table not far away.

"What —" Gaines began.

"Friend of mine — Miss Alla Stimney," Marpe explained.

"Oh! I have heard whispers of that romance, Marpe. I congratulate you. She's a splendid-looking woman!"

"I do not know the man with her, but I'll have to step over and say a word," Marpe said. "I may not get a chance to see her again until I return from Kansas City."

He started to get out of his chair. Miss Alla Stimney

turned her head and saw him. The expression of her face did not change. No hint of recognition came into it. She raised her right hand and brushed it lightly across her ear three times, as though brushing back a stray lock of hair.

Creighton Marpe resumed his chair and sighed.

"What's the trouble?" Captain Gaines wanted to know. "Change your mind? I'd like to meet her."

"Confound it! She flashed me a signal. 'Do not recognize me,' that signal said."

"So you people go in for all that sort of thing, do you!" asked Gaines.

"Yes, we have out little eccentricities," Marpe admitted. "There are times when we need our little signals. We have —"

Once more he ceased speaking abruptly, and Captain Gaines glanced quickly at Alla Stimney. Now she was holding the lobe of her right ear between thumb and forefinger as she smiled at the man sitting across the table from her.

"Any meaning to that?" Gaines asked.

"Yes," Marpe replied. "She is telling me to follow her when she leaves the café."

CHAPTER III

BOUND WEST

They finished their luncheon, paid their check, tipped the waiter handsomely, lighted smokes, and pretended a conversation regarding business so that they could loiter without arousing suspicion. Alla Stimney did not look their way again. She was conducting an animated conversation with her escort.

Creighton Marpe and Captain Gaines inspected the man well from the near distance. He was of middle age, amble as to girth and florid of face. He had a sleek, prosperous appearance, and seemed to exude the thought that he was a sort of oily individual. Marpe's blood boiled at the manner in which he looked at Alla Stimney as he bent across the table.

"Never saw the scamp before in my life," Gaines said.

"Nor have I," said Marpe.

"Yes; and he acts like one who has just made his first killing in the market," Marpe added.

"Do you suppose, Marpe, that he is concerned in this affair upon which you are engaged?"

"I haven't the slightest idea," Marpe replied. "Many strange things happen in the Service. Miss Stimney gave me that signal, and it cannot be ignored. There — he is paying his check. We'll get out and pick them up as they leave."

They left the café, descended the steps to the main

lobby of the big hostelry, and there waited in the ever-changing crowd. A short time later, Alla Stimney and her escort descended the steps and passed within a short distance of them.

"I must send a telegram," Alla Stimney told the man beside her, in such a tone that Marpe could hear.

"There is a telegraph desk just across the lobby, dead lady," her escort replied.

Creighton Marpe ground his teeth in rage. "Dear lady" was one of his pet modes of address when he talked to Alla Stimney. He felt like resenting the remark forcibly, especially when Alla glanced at him with her eyes twinkling, showing that she knew Marpe had heard. But the Service came first. So Marpe followed the pair at a short distance, Captain Gaines walking beside him and talking in a natural manner about nothing much at all.

Alla Stimney led her escort to the telegraph counter, and he stepped back politely and stood surveying the crowd while she picked up a pencil and reached for a message blank. But she seemed to be unable to decide just what to write. She looked at the wall as though thinking deeply, and tapped nervously with the pencil on the counter.

"Um!" Marpe grunted, suddenly. He moved a step nearer, and Captain Gaines went along with him. They, too, seemed to be merely watching the crowd — but Creighton Marpe was listening intently to the erratic tapping of the pencil in the hand of Alla Stimney.

It was the telegraph code that she was using, making the dots and dashes as she tapped the counter with the pencil. Marpe interpreted it readily:

"Take — good — look — at — him. He — is — one — of — them. Name — is — Herman — Carlmurg. That — is — all."

Then she turned and looked straight at him, her own

face expressionless. Marpe would have started toward her, but once more she gave him the signal not to recognize her. And then she gave him yet another, which meant that he was to go his own way and attend to his own business.

She crumpled the telegraph blank and turned toward Herman Carlmurg again and touched him on the arm. Together they left the hotel. Marpe and Gaines, following, saw them get into a taxicab and drive away. Marpe hurried to the cab starter, exhibited his badge of authority and asked one question: "Where did they go?"

"Metropolitan Museum of Art," the starter replied.

"What do you think of that?' Marpe asked Gaines, as they went down the street. "Going to the Museum. She flashed me the message that the man was one of them, and that his name is Herman Carlmurg."

"I'll remember Herman," Captain Gaines declared.

"So shall I," Marpe assured him. "She is keeping an eye on him, I suppose. Well, Gaines, we'll walk down the street and get some railroad tickets now."

"Going to sneak it?" Gaines wanted to know.

"No, sir! My foes know that I am going to Kansas City, so why pretend otherwise? I'll not be in much danger until that document is in my possession."

"But they might keep you from getting to Kansas City," Gaines pointed out.

"That would only delay matters a bit. If anything happened to me, another man would be sent."

"They may be able to handle another man easier. Confound it, Marpe, you are entirely too modest!"

"I may say," Marpe replied, "that I do not intend to sleep much. I'll be alert, naturally."

They walked down a cross street to a railroad ticket office where Marpe sought certain information and then purchased tickets.

"It occurs to me that you are going to do considerable traveling," Gaines remarked. "Three tickets, a lower berth and a drawing-room, eh? Going to take along a party? What is this — a lodge excursion?"

"I am to be the entire party," Marpe replied. "I'm leaving this evening, and I'll be in Chicago tomorrow evening in time to catch a limited train to Kansas City, where I'll arrive the next morning. And I intend to get some sleep tonight. I may not be able to get much for some time thereafter."

"Going to sleep all over the Pullman car?" Gaines asked. "And why so many tickets?"

"You have to hold two to get a drawing room, as you perhaps know, and one for a lower berth."

"I know that. But —"

"And I like to patronize the railroads," Marpe added.

"Kind sir, your tone tells me that I am to attend to my own business," Captain Gaines said. "I'll try to do so."

"Stop long enough to light a cigarette! Glance toward the front of the office," Marpe whispered. "There is our friend, Mr. Lenserg."

"Why, so it is!" Gaines agreed, looking over the flaming match. "Rather persistent devil, isn't he? Still on the trail, and all that."

"And he'll probably continue to trail," Marpe said.

"Suppose that I pick a fight with him and you slip away during the fuss."

"Wouldn't do any good in the long run," Marpe explained. "I've got a better way than that. Come right along with me."

Creighton Marpe led the way to the front of the big office, where the man Lenserg was pretending to be looking at some railroad folders.

"Ah, Mr. Lenserg, we meet again!" Marpe said. "I told you once that your mere presence made me nervous, so you should remain away from me. However, you are only trying to do your work, and every man has his work to do. And I am going to save you some trouble."

"Indeed?" Lenserg said.

"Yes, sir! I'm going to give you all the information you require, so you won't have to trouble of finding it out for yourself. I am going to leave the city by train at five o'clock today, my destination being Kansas City."

"Thanks," Lenserg said, sarcastically. "And from which station, may I ask?"

"Oh, you may ask! From the Grand Central Station, my dear sir. I have Lower Six in the car behind the club car. Probably we can have a rubber of bridge."

"It takes four persons to have a proper rubber of bridge," Lenserg insinuated.

"Yes. I take it that you may have a friend aboard," Marpe said, with meaning.

"And am I to assume that you may be able to scare up a friend also?" Lenserg asked, also with meaning.

"Stranger things have happened," Marpe admitted. "Always liable to meet a friend on a train. I may mention that when I am traveling I am very alert. There seems to be something about the clickety-clack of the car wheels that makes me snappy. I am awake and wary, if you catch my meaning. I am rather particular about my diet, smoke only my own cigars and cigarettes, and am a very light sleeper."

"Interesting facts," Lenserg observed.

"I do not carry a cane with me on such trips, hence rapier practice is denied me. But I dearly love an automatic pistol, and I always carry one."

"And are you a good shot?" Lenserg inquired.

"Man! You should see me mow 'em down!" said Creighton Marpe.

He laughed and turned away with a grinning Captain Gaines at his heels. Once more they hailed a taxicab, and started to journey uptown to the apartment house where Marpe had a bachelor suite.

Marpe packed a bag, and then they sat and talked and smoked until the proper hour arrived, when they started downtown again. At Grand Central Station, Marpe showed one ticket and the lower berth check to the gate man, bade farewell to Gaines, and hurried aboard the train.

He was conducted to his car and seat. He opened his bag and got out a traveling cap and some cigars. Then he sat back and viewed the arriving passengers in quite a normal manner, to all outward appearances. But he really was watching closely, trying to search out his unknown foes if there were any aboard.

He did not see Lenserg. He assumed that Lenserg would not be on the train since his identity was known to Marpe, but that there would be somebody else Marpe did not know by sight.

Just before the train started, Marpe got up and went into the club car ahead, where he made himself comfortable with cigar and newspaper. But he sat in a corner seat from which he could view the entire interior of the car.

CHAPTER IV

OUTWITTED

When dinner was called, Creighton Marpe went to the dining car and ate a substantial meal. The diner was crowded, and if he had foes there he was unable to identify them as such. They would be clever, he knew; not the sort to betray by furtive actions that they were other than innocent travelers.

He left the diner and started back through the train, searching for the Pullman conductor, and finally locating him sitting in one of the cars and going over his lists.

"Kindly follow me into the vestibule," Marpe said, speaking in low tones and stopping for an instant beside the seat as though trying to maintain his balance in the swaying train. "It is very important."

He went on without once glancing at the conductor, who arose presently and followed him. Marpe was standing back in a dark corner of the vestibule between the two cars.

"I am a government man on official duty, and may have enemies aboard the train," Marpe explained, swiftly. "I have Lower Six in the can behind the club car, and a drawing-room in the car behind that. Here are the tickets covering the drawing-room. Please have the porter make up both the upper and lower berths and hang the curtains. Explain to him only as much as is necessary."

"I understand, sir," the conductor said. "You don't

want everybody to know where you'll sleep."

"Exactly!" Marpe replied. "I haven't quite decided. I'll be governed by circumstances."

"Anything I can do to help?" the conductor wanted to know.

"Thanks, no! This is the sort of game that we play without outside help," Marpe explained.

He started on through the train, secure in the knowledge that nobody had witnessed his short conversation with the Pullman conductor. He came, after a time, to a compartment car, and started walking briskly along the wide side aisle.

A woman appeared at the other end of the aisle and approached him, a woman of perhaps thirty, fashionably attired, well groomed, of the sort generally to be found on limited trains. She seemed to be on her way to the diner.

When only a few feet separated Marpe and the woman, the latter suddenly lurched to one side, grasped at the handrail, and started to fall. Marpe sprang forward and supported her.

"My ankle!" she gasped, her face twisting as though with pain. "I — I turned it."

"Ankles are treacherous things at times," Marpe said, smiling down at her.

"I'd have fallen, I believe, if it hadn't been for you."

"Nonsense! You caught the rail neatly. But I am glad that I was at hand and could be of service."

"I wonder if I could bother you a bit. I have a compartment in the next car. If you would be kind enough to assist me there, I'd appreciate it."

"Certainly," Marpe told her. "But perhaps you can continue in a moment. A twisted ankle hurts fiendishly for a time, and then is better."

"I feel half ill," she complained. "I can have some dinner sent in to me."

Creighton Marpe assisted her to the end of the car and opened the door and helped her out into the vestibule. His eyes made swift search of the dark recesses of that vestibule before he ventured into it, but found it empty. He opened the opposite door and aided her into the car and to the door of the compartment she designated.

"Thank you," she said. "Would you care to come in a moment?"

"I believe not," Marpe said, firmly.

"I am a bit lonesome, and you seem to be the sort of man that a woman would like to talk to."

"No doubt a conversation with you would be interesting," Marpe said. "If you care to go to the observation car —"

"The proprieties?" she questioned, laughing a bit. "We'll leave the door open. And I do not feel like walking through the train to the observation car. My ankle, you know."

"Ah, yes, your ankle," Marpe said. "Ankles are treacherous things, as I observed, and also convenient things at time. More romances have started from a sprained ankle — real or pretended —"

"So you are afraid of a romance? We can avoid that, can't we?" she asked.

"Certainly," he said. "Does the ankle hurt much now? I thought not."

"Do you mean to insinuate that I pretended to turn my ankle just to strike up an acquaintance with you?"

"Certainly! Didn't you?" Marpe said. "You see, madam, I caught sight of you peeking around the corner of the aisle as I entered that compartment car. And as soon as you saw me, you entered the aisle and started toward me — and sprained your ankle."

She laughed again. "Perhaps that is true. Am I so very wicked, using that means to strike up an acquaintance with an interesting man, when I am so lonesome?"

"That interesting man stuff would catch nice out of ten, but I happen to be the tenth," Marpe told her. "By the way, let me ask you something. Did you ever hear of Lenserg?"

He fired the question at her in such a manner that she was caught utterly off guard. A slight twist of her lips, the ghost of a frown, a tiny start betrayed her.

"I see that you have," Marpe continued. "Friend of your probably. Need we say more?"

"You think that you are very clever," she said.

"Dear me, no! That is not cleverness. It was all so obvious, if you'll pardon me for saying so. I really expected to meet foes more worthy."

With that, Creighton Marpe left her standing there and continued his journey through the train. He went to the club car and resumed his seat in a corner, and this time he perused a magazine. But he did not lose himself in the story he was reading to such an extent that he neglected to remain alert.

However, nobody made an effort to engage him in conversation, nobody seemed to be watching him. One by one, men left the club car and went to their berths. And finally Creighton Marpe closed the magazine, politely stifled a yawn, glanced at his wristwatch, and left his seat.

He went slowly the length of the car and into the car behind. The porter had made up the berths and the aisle was curtained. Marpe got into Lower Six and prepared for the night. Finally, he stretched out in the berth and turned off the light.

But he did not go to sleep. He had no intention of sleeping in that berth, where he might be caught off guard and prove to be an easy victim. He remained there quietly until about midnight, when he got into a light dressing-gown, put on slippers, and crawled between the curtains.

He started down the aisle of the swaying car, brushing against the curtains, squeezing to one side once to allow a trainman to pass. When he came to the end of the car he kept going, out into the vestibule and across it, into the car behind, and to the drawing-room that had been prepared for him.

Lights were burning in the drawing-room, and it took Marpe only an instant to make sure that no foe lurked there. So he locked the door and began a more methodical inspection of the room. There was nothing to indicate that an intruder had been in the place.

Everything seemed to be all right. But Marpe took the bed in the upper berth apart and remade it carefully. He had heard of such things as the prick of a hidden needle inducing a drugged sleep. Satisfied at last that his enemies, if they were on the train and active against him, had not tampered with anything in the drawing-room, Marpe got into the upper berth, made himself comfortable, pulled the curtains together, and turned off the light.

"*Feliz aventura!*" Marpe muttered. "Happy adventure, huh? Maybe it will be, and maybe not. You never can tell in a case like this."

He was asleep within a sort time. And evidently he had taken all his precautions for naught, for he was not molested during the night. It was about dawn when he awoke, inspected the luminous dial of his watch to get the time, and crawled cautiously out of the berth.

He slipped into his dressing-gown, clutched the automatic in the pocket, unlocked and opened the door. The Pullman conductor sprang out of a seat only a few feet away.

"I've been keeping an eye on your drawing-room, sir," the conductor said.

"Thanks! But was it necessary for you to go to all that

trouble?" Marpe asked.

"Well, there were a couple of gents prowling through the train like they were looking for somebody who was missing. They are passengers and didn't create any disturbance, so I couldn't jump them about it. They saw that I had an eye on them, though, and stopped it."

"Um!" Marpe grunted. "Did you know the gentlemen?"

"Never saw them until this trip, and I've been on this run for quite a few years. They've got a compartment in the car where you reserved a lower."

"Thanks. I'll look 'em over," Marpe said.

He went across the vestibule and into the car forward, where he parted the curtains of Lower Six carefully. He found what he had rather expected to find — the contents of his bag scattered all over the berth.

Marpe chuckled as he returned the things to the bag, collected his clothes and dressed. He went to the washroom to finish dressing, packed the bag neatly afterward, locked it, put it beneath his berth, and went forward to the club car.

It was only an hour after dawn, but there were passengers in the club car. In one corner were four men who had spent the entire night playing bridge, probably for high stakes. And there were tow others who sat side by side and smoked.

Creighton Marpe gave them a swift look and sat down opposite them. He pulled at a cigarette and watched the scenery rushing past. He watched the men across the aisle, too. Something seemed to tell him that they were foes; some unusual sense warned him to be alert. And he could be now, after a refreshing sleep. He glanced up quickly to find one of them men glaring at him, and then he felt sure. Marpe smiled in a knowing way and looked through the window again.

"My friend, you look as though had had a good

night," one of the men said to Marpe.

"Never slept better, sir," Marpe replied. "But you and your friend look as though you haven't slept at all, if you'll pardon me for saying so."

"Only fitfully," the other replied.

"Possibly a troubling conscience," Marpe told him. "You might take a nap during the day. I'll not, of course."

There could be no mistaking his meaning. One of the men glared and the other almost snarled at him.

"It'll be a lonesome day," Marpe continued. "Not very much excitement on a trip like this. Though I did meet a charming lady."

"Some men have all the luck," one of them answered.

"She was inclined to get better acquainted with me, too. A charming lady, but I felt compelled to avoid her. You see, she knows Lenserg."

"Lenserg?" one questioned.

"Yes, Lenserg — the man under whose direction you two are working. She probably knows Herman Carlmurg, too."

"You appear," said the man across the aisle, "to be exceedingly wise."

"Oh, not exceedingly so!" Marpe protested. "Only moderately wise. By the way, while you were searching my bag, you uncorked my shaving powder. Dreadful mess!"

"Are you accusing us —"

"Tut, tut!" said Marpe. "What is a little face powder between friends? And you certainly annoyed the Pullman conductor, too. I imagine he thought you were bandits. Thanks, however, for not breaking into the drawing-room I was occupying and ruining my sleep. Now I believe that I shall go and have an early breakfast. See you later, gentlemen!"

CHAPTER V

OUTWITTED AGAIN

That evening when the train reached Chicago, Creighton Marpe took his time about leaving it, and allowed his foes to go ahead of him through the gates. He caught sight of the woman, alone, and of the two men he had met in the club car.

He had almost four hours between trains in Chicago and a change of stations to make. He did not know how many were arrayed against him, and if there was anybody at hand to aid him in a pinch he did not know that. For no member of the Service had approached to signal him that a comrade was in the neighborhood.

He continued to be alert. He went through the station crowd, carrying his bag, descended to the street level, and engaged a taxicab to drive him to the other station. There he checked his bag and went to the restaurant to spend considerable time over his dinner.

When he had finished eating, he still had an hour before the train would be open. He prowled through the waiting rooms, scrutinizing those in the crowd. This was the part of his work that Marpe disliked — the inactive part where he was compelled to be on guard constantly and he was denied a clash, either verbal or physical, with his foes.

Standing near the entrance to the station, he saw the woman again. She got out of a taxicab and went through the station, a porter carrying her bag. A short time later, the two men arrived. They passed into the station without seeing Marpe.

Marpe knew that the westbound limited was to run in two sections. He visited a Pullman officer, identified himself, and got space on both sections. And then he waited until the gates were thrown open.

He showed himself so that the others could see him. He fussed around the newsstand, purchasing magazines and fruit, and so gave them the chance to pass through the gate ahead of him. He went through a moment later.

Now he was watching them closely, through he pretended not to be, and he knew that they were watching him. Marpe went along the second section, found his car, showed his transportation, and gave his bag to the porter, who carried it inside.

Through a window he watched the others as they boarded the second section also. He caught a station porter who was just leaving the car, gave him his bag and a dollar, and told him to take the bag to a certain berth in the first section of the train on the next track.

Then Marpe walked through the train to the club car. He saw the two men in a compartment which had the door open, but acted as though he had not seen. The woman was not in evidence, and Marpe supposed that she was in one of the compartments.

He went to the club car, struck a match and ignited a cigar, and paced back and forth like a man eager for the train to start. His two enemies entered, glared at him, and sat down to smoke and watch him. Marpe gave them not the slightest attention.

He glanced through the windows now and then at the first section. And suddenly he darted through the door of the car, sprang to the platform, raced across it, and jumped upon that first section just as it started pulling out of the station. Standing on the steps, Creighton Marpe looked back and thumbed his nose at the two enraged men on the other train. "Compliments from The Man Who Changed Rooms," he shouted to them.

Now he was safe from annoyance for a time, he believed. He was on the first section of the train, and they were on the second. And those sections would not be together for some time. So Marpe claimed his berth, opened his bag, and made himself comfortable.

He had speech with the train conductor later in the evening and ascertained that the two sections would be side by side at three o'clock in the morning at a division point in Iowa. Marpe made certain requests and went to bed. At half past two o'clock the porter woke him, and he dressed swiftly.

The train pulled into the division point for a change of locomotives and crews. Marpe watched carefully. The second section pulled in quietly beside the first. Standing in the deep shadows beside the baggage truck on the platform, Marpe watched his two foes leave the second section and dart across the platform and get upon the first just as it started to pull out. Marpe, grinning, got aboard the second section.

Now the enemy was rushing ahead of him on the first section, and he was safe on the second. And he had enjoyed several hours of sleep. He did not retire now, but went back to the observation car and made a friend of the lonesome flagman.

He watched the dawn come, saw the banners of sunrise in the sky. The train was running on time, nearing Kansas City. Marpe went back into the car where he had a berth and performed his morning ablutions.

Then the station. Marpe dropped off as the train came to a stop, to find that the first section was on the next track. Marpe hurried across to it to get his bag. He came face to face with the two men and nodded pleasantly.

"It appears gentlemen, that we have been on different trains," said Creighton Marpe.

Neither of them had a reply for him. They turned their backs and stalked away from him as he got his bag, which convinced Marpe that somebody else was watching. And when he turned he saw him — Lenserg!

Lenserg here in Kansas City, and Marpe had left him behind in New York, and no trains could beat the ones upon which Marpe had traveled.

Marpe went straight up to him. "So I see your disagreeable face again, do I?" he said.

"As you see."

"Airplane, I suppose."

"Certainly. Been waiting here for quite some time for you."

"Nice of you to give me all these little attentions," Marpe told him. "By the way, I met two interesting gentlemen on the train, also a lady. But none of them was clever enough to be real interesting. Really, Lenserg, you should engage better people."

"I may, at that," Lenserg said.

"And now, Mr. Lenserg," Marpe told him, stepping a bit closer and the expression of his face changing and becoming stern, "let us forget these pleasantries and get right down to business. I understand you and your friends, and you had better understand me. I am on a certain mission, as you know. I have been playing with you, but I play no more. It is business now, Mr. Lenserg! Get in my way now, and I'll tramp on you!"

"The game isn't over," Lenserg said.

"I warned you, Lenserg!"

"Of course, if you call in the police, and the army and navy —"

"Don't need 'em, Mr. Lenserg! Good day!"

Marpe brushed past him and went into the station. He decided to eat breakfast there, and so entered the restaurant and sat at a table. He saw Lenserg glancing at him through one of the windows. He noticed, too, that the waiter who served him was of the same race as Lenserg. He watched the waiter narrowly as the food was brought.

"Took you a long time," Marpe commented.

"Very busy this morning, sir. Sorry!"

"I thought that maybe you'd stopped to talk to somebody," Marpe told him.

The waiter said nothing. Marpe attacked the breakfast. He put sugar and cream in his coffee, stirred it, inhaled the steamy aroma.

"Um!" Creighton Marpe muttered. "Thought so! Lenserg got to him, eh? Never would have noticed the taste, but you can always get it from the odor."

He pretended to drink the coffee, but he did not. At the corner of the table, there was a potted plant, and Marpe watered it with the coffee when he felt certain that there was nobody watching him. He called for his check, in time, gave the waiter an ordinary tip, got up, picked up his bag and put on his hat, and started from the room.

But something seemed to go wrong with Mr. Creighton Marpe at that juncture. He stopped, and weakly brushed one hand across his eyes. A far-away look came into those eyes, too, and Marpe's lower jaw sagged, and he seemed to be breathing with difficulty.

He passed through the doors and made his way to the street in front of the station. He leaned against the building there, dropped his bag to his feet, seemed to grow suddenly weak. His eyes rolled, he clutched his throat with his left hand.

Lenserg suddenly stepped up beside him.

"Marpe, you seem to be quite ill," Lenserg said. "You're in bad shape, man! Better get to your hotel. Let me help you to a cab."

It seemed that Creighton Marpe was trying to speak,

to tell him something, and that he was unable to do so. Lenserg clutched him by the arm, picked up the bag, and urged him forward. Marpe went along with him like a helpless child, seemingly unable to think or act for himself.

Lenserg came to the curb and beckoned the chauffeur of the nearest taxi. The taxi darted forward and stopped, and Lenserg opened the door.

And then Creighton Marpe changed swiftly. He laughed lightly and his face cleared and his eyes twinkled.

"Thanks, Lenserg!" he said. "I'll take my bag now, please. It isn't every day that I have such an aristocratic porter. And, by the way, I didn't drink that coffee."

As Lenserg recoiled, his face purple with wrath, Marpe laughed again and got into the taxi. He slammed the door.

"Hotel Baltimore," he directed the chauffeur.

He laughed again as the taxi wheeled away.

CHAPTER VI

SEVERAL FOES

At the hotel, Creighton Marpe registered under his own name and addressed the clerk: "Got a room and bath for me?"

"Yes, Mr. Marpe. Reserved on telegraph from New York."

"When was the reservation wires?"

"We got it yesterday morning, sir."

"Good enough! And how was the request signed?"

The clerk consulted a file of messages. Signed 'Strecko,' sir," he replied. "Rather unusual signature, but we made the reservation, nevertheless."

"Perfectly all right," Marpe told him. "But I do not want the room; I want another."

"It is a good room, Mr. Marpe."

"Not objecting to it on the grounds that it might not be suitable," Marpe hastened to assure him. "I am on government business. I may have active enemies. That room was assigned to me twenty-four hours ago. Many persons may have learned that I am to have that room."

"Just as you please, Mr. Marpe. I'll give you another."

"I'll go to my room at once, and I expect a caller soon. If anybody asked for me, I'm in."

Marpe ascended in the elevator with a bellhop and was conducted to the room that had been assigned him. The bellhop withdrew. Creighton Marpe made a swift inspection of the closet and bath, finding them both empty. Then he examined the room itself, and became assured that everything was as it should be. After that he paced the floor from one corner of the room to another, waiting.

The telephone rang, and Marpe darted across to it.

"Mr. Marpe?" a man's voice rang.

"Yes."

"Captain Makker speaking."

"Come right up, Captain."

Marpe replaced the telephone receiver on its hook and took up a position in the middle of the room. Once more he glanced around like a man surveying the scene of an impending battle.

He heard an elevator door clang in the distance, and moved swiftly across the room to the door, which he unlocked. His hand went into his coat pocket and clutched the automatic that was there, holding it ready for instant use.

A knock on the door.

"Come in!" Marpe called.

The door was opened, and a man stood framed in it. "You are Mr. Marpe?" he asked.

"I am, yes. And you — ?"

"Captain Makker."

"Ah! Come right on in, Captain, and close the door behind you, please," Marpe instructed. "Have to be a bit careful, you know."

"Naturally," his caller said. "I don't blame you at all for being careful."

"And so, being careful, we'll have you turn the key in the lock of that door, please," Marpe said. "Thank you! Sit down there by the table, now."

Marpe walked around to the other side of the table and stood looking down at him. "You are not in uniform, Captain," he said.

"It would have been conspicuous. I thought it best not to wear one."

"Undoubtedly it was best. There is a penalty for impersonating an officer of the United States Army."

"But how could that apply to me?" the other asked, looking up at him quickly.

"Steady, sir!" Marpe warned. "You'll notice that my right hand is in my pocket. You are covered with an automatic."

"Well, upon my word! This is a reception that I did not expect."

"I dare say. But we have to be careful," Marpe told him. "Got something for me?"

"When I hear a hear a certain password, Mr. Marpe."

"Um! It would be better, under the circumstances, if you spoke that password first," Marpe said. "Just suppose, for the sake of argument, that you are not Captain Makker, but one of the enemy. I speak the password, you get it —"

"But how do I know that you are Creighton Marpe? One of the enemy might have registered under that name in the hope of getting what I have to deliver."

"I know that I am Marpe, you see, but I do not know that you are Captain Makker."

"Oh, well, I guess that is all right! I have a sealed document for you, Mr. Marpe. Here it is."

He brought it from an inside pocket of his waistcoat and put it down on the table. It was an envelope of very thin paper, about five inches square.

"Very good!" Marpe said. "I am to take this thing and get it to New York as swiftly as possible, and put it in the hand of a certain gentleman there."

"That is my understanding. I'll be going, then. You'll be wanting to make your arrangements for the return trip. How do you return, Mr. Marpe?"

"Nobody knows that except myself."

"Beg pardon! Shouldn't have asked. Well, glad to have met you, Marpe. Hope to meet you again when we can have time to chin together."

"Just a moment!" Marpe said. "Sit down again!"

"Beg pardon?"

"I said for you to sit down. Before my trigger finger gets nervous and contracts. That's it. Your hands flat on the table, please."

"I must say —"

"Say nothing! I'll do the talking," Creighton Marpe told him. "Man, your game is raw!"

"What do you mean? Do you realize how you are acting, what you are saying?"

"Certainly! You are not Captain Makker. I have seen a recent photograph of him. Just sit still and do not make a move, if you value your health. We'll have a look at this document you brought me."

Marpe, ever alert, ripped the envelope open and took out several sheets of thin paper.

"Blank!" he said. "Just as I expected, sir. You believed that I would accept this thing and hurry away, back to New York. With me out of the way, the real Captain Makker could not deliver the genuine document. There would be a break in the plans, and you people might have a change to get the thing from Makker. How many more of you are in the hall?"

"You seem to know everything," the other said. "Well, what are you going to do about it?"

"What have you done with Makker?"

"I do not know what has been done with him, if anything," came the reply. "This was just a trick to get to you before Makker did, get you out of the way."

"I should smash you in the nose," Creighton Marpe told him. "But I have neither the time nor inclination for barroom brawls, so to speak. You appreciate the fact that

I could shoot you, say that you intruded here and tried a holdup, or something like that?"

Color drained from the other's face. "I — I suppose that you could," he said.

"You people certainly are eager to get that document, whatever it is. I do not know what it is, nor does my Chief. But I have orders to carry the thing to New York, and I am going to do just that. Now you tell me something — how many men are prowling around in the hall outside, hoping to get at me and steal my credentials?"

"I am not talking."

"Didn't expect you to," Marpe confessed. "However, when you see them again, just tell them that it won't do any good to try to get credentials from me. They couldn't do it. I think that I'll keep you here until I hear from Captain Makker. If anything happened to him, I can deal with you."

"What do you think has happened to him?"

"To be truthful, I do not think that anything much has happened to him, unless he is an utter fool. I do not think he'd come alone from Fort Leavenworth to deliver that document to me. But possibly you people have managed to delay him."

"That's it. Might as well confess. He was to be delayed until I had the chance to hand you that bogus letter and get you started back to New York."

"No doubt you were ready for me in that other room — the room that was reserved for me."

"Naturally."

"Uh-huh! Thought as much," Marpe said.

"You are not yet safe back in New York. You've got a job ahead of you — to get that document, get it to New York, and deliver it safely to a certain person."

"Very simple task," Marpe assured him. "Merely a matter of hours. Steady, there! Hands on the table!"

Creighton Marpe whirled suddenly to one side as he spoke. He had noticed a slight contraction of the other's eyelids. And now he discovered the reason for it.

The door of the room adjoining had been unlocked and opened. A man was creeping upon him. But now the intruder came to an abrupt stop as Marpe drew the automatic from his pocket.

"Steady, both of you!" he warned. "Close that door — you! Come over to the table and sit down. Hands flat! It occurs to me that I may have some target practice here yet."

They sat side by side and glowered at him, two middle-aged men of the type Creighton Marpe expected to find arrayed against him. He stepped across to the door, still alert, and propped a chair beneath the knob.

"Only two doors, thank heavens!" Marpe said. "You gentlemen are rather persistent, aren't you? Steady, now, while I use the telephone." He stepped back to the instrument and put the receiver to his ear.

"Get the house detective up here quick!" he snapped into the transmitter.

Replacing the receiver, he approached the table again.

"I simply cannot be bothered anymore by you men," he told his prisoners. "Expecting a caller, you know. If isn't at all gentlemanly of you to annoy me in this manner."

"Oh, we'll go!" said the latest arrival.

"I know that. You'll go in charge of the house officer. And possibly you'll be detained for a time, at least until I am sure that nothing has happened to Captain Makker."

Once more there came a knock on the door.

"Who's there?" Marpe questioned.

"House detective, Mr. Marpe!"

"One moment, please!" Marpe, watching his prisoners, went across the room to the door. There was a smile upon his face and it was a peculiar sort of smile. He turned the key and unlocked the door and stepped back swiftly. "Come in!" he called.

The door was opened and a man entered. And the instant he had done so Creighton Marpe slammed the door shut and poked the muzzle of his automatic into the man's ribs.

"Up with your hands!" he snapped. "House detective, are you? One of the gang waiting in the hall, you mean. You heard me telephone and thought that you'd get to me before the house officer arrived. Keep those hands up!"

"You — why — I'm the house officer!"

"If you are, we'll know it later. But I think that you're not. You see, your friends at the table are not very clever. When you spoke and said that you were the house officer, they betrayed in their faces that they knew your voice, and that it was the voice of a friend. Stand right there against the wall, please, and keep your hands up. I feel quite flattered, gentlemen. It appears that they have sent an army against me."

Again there came a knock at the door.

"Who is it?" Marpe demanded.

"House officer, sir."

"Come right in."

Once more a man entered the room. His eyes opened wide at what he saw.

"Ah! Here we have the real house officer," Marpe said. "I spotted him in the lobby when I entered the hotel. Can always tell a hotel detective. And that is another reason why I did not accept the fake one."

CHAPTER VII

THE BACK TRAIL

"What's all this?" the house officer asked.

"Have you been informed as to my business?" Marpe wanted to know.

"Yes, Mr. Marpe."

"Good! These gentlemen are attempting to molest me. Just take them away, so I'll not be annoyed by them anymore."

"Want me to make charges against them?"

"Keep them in the manager's office for a time, until I tell you what to do."

"Very well, sir. I'll telephone for help."

Marpe watched the three while the officer telephoned. Another house detective appeared, and an assistant manager. The men were searched, and weapons taken from them, and they were led away. The assistant manager locked the door that had been opened and was profuse in his apologies.

Marpe was left alone once more. He touched match to cigarette and paced the floor and smoked. Luncheon hour came, and he had something to eat in his room, and was very careful about it, indulging only in a salad that he knew could not have been doctored, plain bread, and water.

He sent down for railroad time tables and consulted them. All he was waiting for now was Captain Makker and the document he was to carry. The instant he got the latter, he would make arrangements for the return trip to New York.

And finally, when he felt that he could endure the delay no longer, he called the army post at Fort Leavenworth by telephone and got the commanding officer on the wire.

"What about Captain Makker?" Marpe asked, after establishing his identity. "I am waiting for him."

"He should be there soon, Mr. Marpe," came the reply. "He started once with a decoy document. They mussed him up a bit and got it away from him. We only hope that they'll think they have the real one."

Marpe chuckled at that. The Army was a bit clever, too, he told himself. He paced the floor some more, not exactly nervous, but restive. Once more the telephone rang.

"Hello!" Marpe called.

"Captain Makker speaking."

"Come right up to the room, Captain. I am waiting for you."

And again Creighton Marpe stood to one side of the door and called for the man who knocked to enter5. He knew at the first glance that this was the genuine Captain Makker.

"I've been having all sorts of fun, Captain," Marpe said. "A fellow impersonated you — unsuccessfully. A couple of others tried to be clever also, and failed."

You have nothing on me," the captain replied. "I was waylaid and knocked out, and papers stolen from me. But a couple of my friends who happened to be near and watching got the men who got me. Just marked them up a bit."

"We'd better conduct the remainder of our conversation in whispers," Marpe said. "The enemy is very active hereabouts. Have you a certain password?"

"Yes. *Feliz* — You may give me the remainder."

"*Aventura!*"

"Fair enough! Here is what you came for."

Captain Makker put a small package down upon the table. It was an envelope about six inches square, of very thin opaque paper, and there was an official seal on it.

"Well, now, that looks like the real thing," Marpe observed. "Not much to cause all this fuss, is it?"

"You don't know what it is?" Captain Makker asked.

"Haven't the slightest idea."

"Nor have I."

"How's that?" Marpe gasped. "What is the confound thing, anyway?"

"I know that it is in code, whatever it is — but sometimes codes are deciphered by the wrong persons."

"I imagined that it was some army stuff you men at Leavenworth had concocted."

"But it isn't. Leavenworth is only a relay station, so to speak," Captain Makker explained. "That thing came to us from the west, presumably the Pacific Coast. You are to carry it on. I do not know what it is, but it sure has had our people worried. We're glad to be rid of it. Six officers in civilian attire were in my neighborhood when I brought it here. Two are outside in the hall now. That's what we think of it."

"Huh! And I've got to carry the thing alone, without any army to guard me," Creighton Marpe said. "With that whole outfit against me, too. Well, makes no difference what it is. None of my business. I've got orders to deliver it to a certain man in New York, and that's all it means to me. Captain, will you be kind enough to wait here for me?"

Creighton Marpe went into the bathroom and closed the door. He was gone about ten minutes. When he emerged, he was grinning like a schoolboy.

"Just tucking the thing away so I can carry it safely," he reported. "And now, Captain Makker, I am going to ask you to do something a bit unethical, as it were."

"What's that?"

"I am going to jump a board bill," Marpe said. "I'll ask you to pay it for me later, however, and here is plenty of money with which to do it. What I mean is, I am going to sneak out of this hotel and leave the enemy holding the sack, if you catch my meaning. And I want you to remain here for at least half and hour after I am gone, and then go downstairs and pay my bill for me."

"I understand, Marpe. Good idea!"

"I'll do some telephoning first, and let us hope that the enemy hears me."

Marpe went to the telephone, consulted the directory, and then called a ticket office.

"I want a lower to Chicago," said he, "on the five o'clock train. Name is Marpe. Yes, sir, I'll claim it at the station in half an hour."

He was smiling as he returned to the table and conducted the conversation in whispers.

"That will cause them to get active, if they heard it," he told the captain.

"But I don't understand. You're tipping them off to what train you'll take."

"Nothing like it! I do not intend to take that train. I am not going to Chicago at all. Nor am I going to catch a train at the Union Station."

He got his bag, put on his hat, and hurried to one of the windows.

"Talk about something, in fairly loud tones," he instructed, speaking in whispers himself.

Captain Makker commenced talking, telling of an incident at Fort Leavenworth, speaking in a loud voice and laughing raucously. And while he did that Creighton Marpe opened the window, making very little noise about it.

"Now, keep muttering," he said, as he shook the captain's hand. "Try to make it sound like a conversation. You grasp the idea? You may have a couple of friends in the hall, but some of the enemy may be in an adjoining room. Goodbye, Captain, and I hope that we meet again."

Creighton Marpe got out upon a fire-escape landing and went swiftly down the ladder to the floor below. He glanced through the window there and saw an empty room. He opened the window and got inside, went to the telephone, spoke in low tones, and asked that one of the house officers be hurried up to him.

The officer was there almost immediately, and Marpe let him in.

"I wondered who was calling from this room," the detective said. "Tried to tell the switchboard girl that she had made a mistake, since this room was not occupied."

"I'm sneaking out," Marpe said, grinning. "Captain Makker will pay my bill in half an hour or so. I want you to help me get out without being seen."

"Come along with me, Mr. Marpe. It is only a step to one of the service elevators."

Marpe followed the house officer into the hall and along it for a short distance, where they disappeared through a door. A moment later, they were in the service elevator and descending to the basement. Arriving there, the officer conducted Marpe to an alley door, and left him there while he went out and got a taxicab and had it ready at the mouth of the alley. Marpe scurried out and got into the cab.

But he did not drive to the Union Station. He went swiftly away from the central part of the city, and finally reached a suburban railroad station. There he dismissed the taxi and hurried into the depot.

And presently a train thundered in, and Creighton Marpe got aboard. He sought the Pullman conductor and acquired a berth. He was on a train bound for St.

Louis instead of one going to Chicago, and at St. Louis he could transfer to a New York train.

Making himself comfortable in the seat Marpe relaxed. He was doubly alert and on guard, now that he was carrying that precious document. He could go, without sleep until he reached New York, if necessary, and he probably would.

He allowed himself to dream a bit of Alla Stimney now. He was eager for her to quit the Service, but she did not want to do so while he remained in it. And he hated to give it up, even to marry Alla Stimney. He loved the thrill of it, the excitement and adventure, the pitting of wits against clever foes.

He felt that he was safe now, that he had escaped the enemy. He knew that there might be a bad moment in New York. They would be watching Major Sinlon, probably, and would make a last effort to get that document. But that was something to worry about when the time came.

The hours passed slowly for Marpe. He read and he smoked, and he watched the scenery through the window until the darkness came. He dined carefully and well. This train was due in St. Louis about midnight, and there was an excellent New York connection. He would make that, he promised himself, and settled down to the last lap of the journey.

As the train pulled into St. Louis, Marpe picked up his bag after motioning the porter aside, and prepared to get off. He wanted to get a compartment on the New York train, if it was possible. He sprang to the platform and hurried along it in the midst of a horde of passengers. He passed through the exit gate and went speedily toward the ticket office. If he made this connection, he would have less than twenty minutes in St. Louis.

He had no trouble getting his compartment. Taking his ticket and change, he turned away from the window — and came face to face with Lenserg.

"Ha. The man who changes rooms," was Lenserg's greeting.

Marpe was startled, though he did not betray it.

"It appears that I run across you every now and then," Marpe said. "Airplane again?"

"Surely! You are not so clever as you think, Mr. Marpe. We had men watching every train, and when you were located on the St. Louis train my man wired back to me. So I came ahead to wait for you."

"You are getting to be a confounded nuisance," Marpe informed him. "I feel inclined to adopt stringent measures regarding you. I cannot be annoyed much more without losing my temper."

"You haven't completed your mission yet, Marpe."

"Merely a matter of time," Marpe assured him. "I suppose you saw me buy my tickets?"

"Yes. I know that you got a compartment, too."

"Going to travel on the same train."

"Possibly."

"Uh-huh! And about how many little playmates are going to be along?" Marpe asked.

"How many have you?" Lenserg countered.

"Have you spotted any?" Marpe wanted to know. "If you haven't anything more important to do, you might do that — try to spot them."

He turned away abruptly and made for the gate, knowing well that Lenserg was close behind him. Lenserg continued to be close behind him as he walked alongside the train, searching for the car in which he had the compartment. It was rather annoying, but Marpe was lightly humming a little air as he mounted the steps in the wake of a porter. He beheld Lenserg making for the Pullman conductor, and guessed that the enemy did not have a reservation, and was compelled to get one at the last moment.

Marpe went into his compartment and closed the door. He opened a window and watched Lenserg conduct negotiations with the Pullman conductor. He saw Lenserg get into a car some distance ahead.

Then Creighton Marpe violated the rules of the railroad company. Picking up his bag, he left the compartment and went into the vestibule, and when the porter was not looking he opened the door and trap on the off side. He dropped down and walked the next track toward the rear of the train.

As he came to the end, the train started. It went without him — but it carried Lenserg.

CHAPTER VIII

TRAPPED

Creighton Marpe returned to the station. There were other trains for New York, and he had to wait only an hour to catch the next. He purchased a compartment and another ticket, turning in the old one. The ticket agent lifted his eyebrows at him.

"Government business — no explanations necessary," Marpe said.

He made his getaway on that train, made himself comfortable in the compartment, and wondered what Lenserg was doing. He did not anticipate any more trouble until he reached New York. But he would not relax vigilance.

The following day, Creighton Marpe sacrificed speed for safety. He lost a couple of hours by leaving the train at a town in Ohio and catching another on a different road. He encountered no opposition. None of his enemies seemed to be around, and he hoped that he had shaken them off.

But they would be massed and waiting for him in New York, and especially at the Hotel Magnificent, he supposed. They undoubtedly had learned of the room he had reserved there several days before, and probably had made certain plans.

And when New York was reached, he did not go into the Grand Central Station, but left the train at a suburban depot. Nor did he go to his rooms. He engaged a cab and hurried to the Hotel Magnificent.

He reported his arrival immediately to the clerk and claimed his room, but he did not go up to it. He checked his bag at the parcel stand and went to sit in an easy chair in the lobby not far from the information desk.

"Hope that I don't have to wait here all day to get some action," he mused.

The ever-changing lobby crowd was all about him, engulfing the chair he was occupying. Creighton Marpe watched it come and go. He did not see any known enemies, nor did he see any known friends. But he made a close observation of every person who approached the information desk.

And then he saw Alla Stimney. The flickering of her eyelids told Marpe that she was surprised to see him then and there. He started to get to his feet, but once more she made that little signal — that he was not to recognize her.

Marpe wondered at that. She seemed to be alone, to be waiting for somebody. She moved slowly through the crowd, and finally sat down at a distance.

Marpe divided his attention now between Alla Stimney and the information desk. And after a time he saw a man stop in front of Alla Stimney and engage her in conversation. The man was Herman Carlmurg.

Marpe remembered Herman, and that Alla had tapped him a message that the man was one of their foes. What was she doing; what sort of game she was playing, Marpe could not guess. He caught her eye, and again she flashed him the message that he was not to recognize her.

However, he did get up and moved slowly around the lobby, and finally came to a stop a few feet from her, where he turned to look over the crowd.

"I am sorry that our luncheon engagement must wait, dear lady," Herman Carlmurg was telling her. "I am wondering if we cannot make it an hour from now. Can't you shop, or something?"

"You are not very gallant," Alla told him.

"I appreciate that fact, and so I'll have to explain. I have been waiting for several days to see a man on very important business. He has just got to the hotel, and I must interview him at once. It should not take me more than an hour."

"I'll wait around the lobby," she said. "If you'll kindly get me a magazine —"

Herman smiled at her and hurried toward the newsstand. Marpe moved a couple of steps nearly, but did not even look down at her.

"Creighton! Don't turn, but listen!" he heard her say in guarded tones. "He is one of them. I have been trying to learn their plans but have not been able to do so. But I am quite sure that they have planned something."

"Do you know Major Sinlon by sight?" Marpe asked.

"Yes," she replied.

"He probably will go to the information desk when he comes in, to see whether I have arrived," Marpe said. "Watch for him. Hold him here in the lobby until I have you paged."

He moved away quickly then, for Herman Carlmurg was coming back toward her with a couple of magazines in his hand. Mr. Carlmurg was much interested in Alla Stimney, Marpe thought, with a pang of jealousy, but had not been interested enough to betray his plans to her.

Marpe went to the parcel counter and got his bag. He gave it to the bellhop, and they ascended to the room Marpe had reserved. As soon as the boy had gone, Marpe made a swift inspection of that room. The closet and bathroom looked innocent enough. There was a door that opened into an adjoining room, and Marpe propped a chair beneath that knob of that. He made sure, then, that his automatic was ready for use, and waited.

The telephone rang. Marpe answered.

"Is this Mr. Marpe?" a man's voice demanded.

"It is, yes."

"Major Sinlon calling. Shall I come right up?"

"Please, Major!"

Creighton Marpe replaced the telephone receiver and hurried across to the hall door. He opened it and peered out into an empty hall. He went out, closed the door behind him, and darted twenty feet to a cross hall and disappeared from view.

He did not have long to wait until a man left the elevator and came briskly along the hall. He stopped in front of the door of Marpe's room and knocked. When he got no answer, the knock was repeated. He seemed puzzled when the door was not opened for him. Out went a hand to try the knob. He found the door unlocked, and opened it.

Marpe slipped quickly along the hall, then, and into the room behind the other. The intruder whirled as Marpe stared to close the door.

"Ah! You are Mr. Marpe?" he asked.

"I am, yes. May I ask by what right you open the door to my room and enter?"

"I just telephoned you from the lobby, and you told me to come up. When you did not answer my knock, I was afraid that — that something had happened to you."

"Oh! You are Major Sinlon?"

"Certainly! I have come for — well, you know what."

Marpe had closed the door, and now he turned the key in the lock and motioned his guest toward a chair. The other sat down.

"I am glad that you got through with it, Mr. Marpe," he said. "We have been worried."

"No doubt," Marpe told him. "Just what is it that you are speaking about?"

"Cautious, aren't you? You are to be complimented on that. It pays to be cautious and alert in this sort of affair."

"True words!" Marpe told him.

"What I am after is a certain document that you got from Captain Makker in Kansas City and have brought to me."

"No doubt that is what you want," Marpe told him. "But how do I know you are the man supposed to receive it?"

"Still cautious? Well, I do not blame you. I am Major Sinlon, I say."

"There is a certain password —"

"Surely! *Feliz Aventuro.*"

"I beg your pardon? Say it slowly, please."

"*Feliz Aventuro,*" the other replied.

"Would you mind spelling it for me, slowly and carefully?"

The other did so, and repeated the spelling at Marpe's request.

"And are you satisfied, Mr. Marpe?" he wanted to know.

"Yes, I am satisfied — that you are an impostor!" Marpe told him.

"What is this, sir? Are you inclined to be facetious? Kindly remember that this is a serious business."

"Very serious," Marpe told him. "So serious that you, sir, are going to sit perfectly still until we got into the matter." Marpe brought forth his automatic, and the expression in his face was that of a grim and determined man.

"Why all this melodrama?" the other demanded. "Have I not given the password?"

"You have given it to me wrong."

"That is the one given me."

"Your Spanish is rotten," Marpe told him. "You said *Feliz Aventuro*. The last letter, my dear sir, is an 'a' and not an 'o.' Lenserg should have sent a man who knows Spanish."

"Why you —"

"Careful! You make a move, and this little toy I am holding will bark at you."

"You are making a mistake, Mr. Marpe. Your superiors shall learn of this."

"If they do, I'll probably have my salary raised," Marpe said.

"I may have made a slight mistake."

"It was not a slight one."

"An easy one to make. I do not know Spanish. And because I get one little letter wrong —"

"That's only one little item. Major Sinlon is a graduate of West Point and certainly studied Spanish there. I have seen the major's photograph, and you do not resemble it in the slightest degree. More over, I happen to know that your name is Herman Carlmurg! By the way, has Lenserg got back to town yet?"

Herman Carlmurg sat back in his chair, wrath showing in his face as Marpe laughed at him.

"Very good, Mr. Marpe!" he said. "You take another trick in the game. But the game is not yet ended."

"It is for you, I fear."

"What are you going to do? Turn me over to the police?"

"That isn't being done under the circumstances," Marpe said. "But I'd advise you to sit still and not try any funny tricks, or I may turn you over to some hospital."

"For what are we waiting?"

"To see whether Lenserg or any of the others show up," said Marpe. "I have a lot of fun with Lenserg. I understood that he was quite a dangerous person, but I have not found him so."

"As I said a moment ago, the game is not ended."

"I heard you then, and I hear you now."

"You are of the opinion, sir, that you hold the winning hand. But you do not. Let me tell you something — you'll hand that document to me, or you'll never leave his room alive!"

"Isn't that threat rather preposterous?"

"I think not. You have walked into a trap, Mr. Marpe. If you will look at the wall to your left, just beneath the picture, you will see a hole in the wall. It has been there for a couple of days, ever since we engaged the adjoining room. There was a plug in the hole, but you'll notice that it had been withdrawn, and the muzzle of an automatic is through that hole now, Mr. Marpe, covering you effectually. Drop your gun, or my friend will shoot!"

CHAPTER IX

A DECISION TO BE MADE

Herman Carlmurg was speaking the truth. Marpe saw instantly that whoever was hold that weapon could fire and get him before he could spring far enough to one side to avoid the bullet. He had been trapped neatly.

But he had rather expected that. He had not known what sort of a trap it would be, but he judged that the enemy had had time to prepare one.

"You see?" Carlmurg was saying. "The game is not ended."

"So it seems," Marpe admitted.

"Drop the gun instantly!"

Marpe allowed his automatic to drop to the carpet.

"Stand back!"

Marpe stood back. Herman Carlmurg got up, stepped forward quickly, and picked up the gun.

"Now you may sit down, Mr. Marpe, and keep your hands on the table before you," Carlmurg instructed. "It probably is not necessary to inform you that I'll shoot if you make a hostile move. We are playing for big stakes, remember."

"I do not know anything about it," Marpe complained. "I don't even know what that document is. What's the next move?"

"Sit still. We will make the next move," Carlmurg said.

As he finished speaking, he stepped to the door and unlocked it. Marpe noticed that the muzzle of the automatic no longer menaced him from the hole in the wall. In a moment somebody knocked at the door, and Carlmurg moved back to it, continually watching Marpe, and opened it a crack and peered out. An instant later, Lenserg was in the room.

"You see me again, Marpe," Lenserg said. "Didn't expect that, did you? You have led us a merry chase and I admire you for it, but we have you now, here at the end of the trail. I hope that you will be sensible."

"Just how am I to be sensible?" Marpe asked.

"You know what we want. Give it to us, and you may go."

"Now, Lenserg, you know the game better than that! It wouldn't be playing it if I handed you what you want without any argument or an attempt to outwit you."

"I can understand that, Marpe. You want to make it look right to your chief. We're willing to bind and gag you and leave you here. Whatever story you tell, we'll not contradict it. You may say that half a dozen men jumped you, if you like."

"Oh, I couldn't be so deceitful, though half a dozen or more have jumped me since I was given this assignment," Marpe replied.

"Are you going to hand us that paper?"

"I couldn't think of doing such a thing."

"Want us to find it and take it off you — that it? So you'll be able to say that you didn't give it up? Well, I can't blame you. It doesn't look good to fail."

"*Feliz adventua* — happy adventure," Marpe said.

"You are playing for time, but it won't do you any good," Lenserg told him. "You watch him, Carlmurg, and I'll get that document."

"You won't find it," Marpe declared. "Think that I am an unsophisticated fool to pack such a thing around where it could be found readily?"

"You brought it here with you, expecting to hand it over to Major Sinlon, so it is here."

"Not necessarily. And the major is about due to telephone this room, by the way."

"If he does, the call will not be answered," Lenserg said. "Stand up, Marpe, for I am going to search you."

"It's a useless and criminal waste of time, Lenserg. However, if you insist —"

Creighton Marpe stood up. Lenserg stripped off his coat and examined it thoroughly and tossed it aside. The waistcoat came next, and yielded nothing.

"Strip!" Lenserg ordered.

"Oh, I say!" Marpe protested. "I'm telling you that you won't find it on me."

"We are not playing now. Do as I say!"

Marpe realized that he was dealing with desperate men. He removed his garments one at a time, and Lenserg examined them well while Herman Carlmurg watched him and covered him with his own automatic pistol. Finally he was down to his athletic underwear, which did not take much searching.

"Nothing!" Lenserg said.

"How about his traveling bag?" Carlmurg suggested.

Lenserg unlocked the bag and tumbled out its contents. There was nothing unusual about them, just the ordinary traveling things. Lenserg even ripped out the lining and examined the bag for a false bottom or side.

"Nothing!" he reported.

"Make him talk!" Carlmurg snapped.

"I haven't a thing to say," Marpe told them. "I informed you that you couldn't find the thing on me, and you wouldn't believe it. You've had all your work for nothing."

"But you are going to talk. You are going to tell me where to find that document," Lenserg said, his eyes flaming. "It is death for you if you do not. If we have to fail and suffer the consequences, you'll pay for it, Marpe!"

"What can I say?" Marpe asked.

"You brought it here from Kansas City, didn't you?"

"I did, to give to Major Sinlon, as you know."

"But you have not given it to Major Sinlon. We know where Major Sinlon was when you came upstairs. You had not met him since getting back to the city. You talk, Marpe!"

But Creighton Marpe had thought of a way out now. He gulped and pretended to hesitate, and looked up quickly when Lenserg stepped forward menacingly.

"Just suppose," Marpe said, "that I met a friend in the lobby, and that this friend is in the Service. Suppose, also, that I was a bit afraid that I might encounter trouble in this room. Wouldn't it have been the wise thing for me to hand that document to my friend with orders to wait around the lobby until I communicated again?"

"So that's it!" Lenserg exclaimed. "And your friend —"

"A lady."

"So? We want that document, Marpe, and intend to have it. So think fast! Who is the lady?"

"Her name is Alla Stimney."

"What?" Carlmurg cried.

"Exactly," Marpe said, smiling despite his predicament. "You are acquainted with her, Mr. Carlmurg? She has been rather clever, hasn't she, keeping tabs on you? But I scarcely think that you'll go down into the lobby and seize her and make her surrender that paper."

"You never gave it to her, I was with her a short time ago."

"I know it. You left her for a moment to go and buy her some magazines," Marpe said, grinning.

Herman Carlmurg muttered a curse.

"We'll get her up here!" Lenserg said.

"You may depend on one thing, gentlemen — I'll let you shoot me before I have her up here to be affronted, possibly harmed. If you are men of honor, and will give me your word that she will not be molested —"

"Gladly!" Lenserg said. "We do not fight women. All we want is that document."

"She will come to the telephone if I have her paged."

"Then have her paged. Ask her to come to this room at once," Lenserg said.

"Let me get into my clothes," Marpe said.

He thought that he saw a way out now. He dressed as swiftly as possible. He made himself presentable, and then, while Lenserg and Carlmurg watched closely, he crossed the room and sat down at the telephone.

"I wish to have Alla Stimney paged, please," he said. "She is somewhere in the lobby. I'll hold the wire."

Retaining the receiver at his ear, Creighton Marpe reached out in a manner quite natural and picked up a pen from the desk. He tapped the desk with it nervously, tapped his teeth with it, tapped the telephone transmitter. And he began talking to Lenserg and Carlmurg in a rather loud voice.

"Understand, I won't have her hurt," he said. "If you use rough tactics, I'll get you if it takes me years! I'll tell you confidentially that I am interested in the lady above and beyond the fact that we are in the same line of work."

"Do not worry about that," Lenserg said. "You'll do her a favor by telling her to hand that document to us. When she answers that call, tell her to get up her at once."

Creighton Marpe said something more to them, spoke in such a voice that they did not hear Alla Stimney when she called "hello!" into the telephone transmitter downstairs. But Marpe heard her and knew that she was listening.

And, in a manner quite natural, he tapped the transmitter with the penholder, sending dots and dashes to her:

H — E — L — P.

And then he spoke.

"That you, Alla? Can you hear me — and understand?"

"Yes — I understand," she replied.

"Please come up to my room at once. It is Number 675. At once, that's the girl!"

He returned the receiver to the hook and turned to face them.

"You remember — no rough stuff!" he warned.

"She is a wonderful woman. She had me fooled completely," Herman Carlmurg admitted. "I admire her. I give you my word that she'll not be insulted or bothered in any way. We'll get that paper, detain you both for a short time, that is all."

"If Major Sinlon comes —"

"If he calls, nobody will answer the telephone, and he will wait and call again — too late," Lenserg said. "Marpe, I'm feeling pretty good about this. You have quite a reputation; it isn't everybody who can outwit you. But a man can't win all the time."

"I suppose not," Marpe replied.

He was doing some rapid thinking as Lenserg talked. He hoped that Alla had understood fully, that Major Sinlon was with her, and that these men could be outwitted in the end.

Carlmurg went across the room and unlocked the door.

"When she knocks, you'll call to her to enter," he told Marpe. "Let's have it over with as quickly as possible. No use in fighting after the war is ended."

And so they waited for a few minutes longer, Marpe sitting at the little desk and tapping it nervously. He got out a cigarette, lit it, and blew a cloud of smoke toward the ceiling.

"A lot of fuss about a piece of paper," he said. "I think that I'll get some prosaic sort of job."

"Don't let one failure discourage you," Carlmurg advised. "You have had some great successes. You went up against still opposition this time. I am rather surprised that you were not given a lot of help."

"It's a compliment to me that I wasn't, I suppose," Marpe said. "But it might have been better if I'd had a small army around me — as you did."

A knock on the door. Both Carlmurg and Lenserg were on their feet and moving to either side of that door instantly. They motioned to Marpe.

"Come in!" he called.

She opened the door and stepped inside. She gasped when she saw Carlmurg and Lenserg, and would have retreated, but Lenserg closed the door behind her.

"What — what is it?" Alla Stimney gasped.

"First, dear lady, allow me to compliment you," Herman Carlmurg told her. "You fooled me nicely. It is a wonder that I did not tell you secrets."

"But — I don't understand. What is it, Creighton?" she asked Marpe. "You told me to come up here —"

"He was compelled to do so, Miss Stimney," Lenserg put in. "We forced him to reveal that he had given you a certain document for safe-keeping. We want that document, so we had him tell you to come up. Isn't that right, Marpe?"

"That's right," Marpe replied. "You are at liberty to give them any document you have, Alla. They seem to think that they've got us licked this time. As one of these gentlemen told me a few minutes ago, we can't win always."

"How very ridiculous all this is!" she said. "I haven't any document."

"It will avail you nothing to play for time," Carlmurg told her. "We have no wish to resort to violence. But, if we are compelled to do so — ! It would be the part of wisdom for you to hand us that paper at once."

"I have no paper. Which one do you mean?"

"The one Mr. Marpe carried from Kansas City," Lenserg said.

"But I haven't it. I never have had it."

Carlmurg whirled toward Marpe. "You told us that you gave it to her," he accused.

"I believe that I did say so," Marpe replied.

"It was a lie?"

"Oh, do not call it that, please! Just say that it was a subterfuge," Creighton Marpe begged.

"What was your object?"

"To gain time," Marpe replied.

"And where, then, is the document?" Carlmurg demanded.

"Sorry, but I must refuse to tell you that."

"You think that you are so very clever, eh? On the contrary, my dear sir! We have the lady here now, and you have professed a sentimental interest in her. So we have a grip on you, Mr. Marpe! You would dislike to have anything happen to the lady, eh?"

"If you dare —"

"We are desperate men, Marpe. We intend to have that paper. Tell us at once where it is, or —"

"Or what?" Marpe asked.

"Miss Stimney is entirely in our hands, Marpe!"

For a moment, Creighton Marpe had a horrible fear. He glanced at Alla Stimney, but could read no message in her face. He could produce that document despite the fact that they had not found it when they had searched him so well a few minutes ago.

But he did not want to surrender it. And he did not want harm to come to Alla. It was a difficult decision to make. And now there flashed into his mind the words of his Chief: "If there ever comes a time when you must choose between the Service and your sweetheart, you will remember that the Service comes first!"

"Talk!" Lenserg snapped at him in a hard voice.

CHAPTER X

GOODS DELIVERED

Marpe looked at Alla again.

"Do your duty, Creighton, and do not think of me," she said.

"Why be foolish?" Lenserg asked. "Would it not be better to give us what we want? There is no way out. Let us have it at once, Marpe. No more of your subterfuges."

"It is a difficult decision to make," Marpe said.

"The Service comes first, Creighton," Alla Stimney spoke up. "Do not forget that."

"But you, Alla —"

"I would despise you if you thought otherwise."

"Very well!" He faced Lenserg again. "You won't learn anything from me," he continued. "But if you offer harm to Miss Stimney you'll regret it. I'll hunt you down as I would hunt mad dogs. I'll quit the Service and go on your trail!"

"Don't waste time making threats," Carlmurg interrupted. "Are you going to talk and tell us where that document is? I am asking you for the last time."

"And I am answering the same — you'll learn nothing from me," Marpe said.

Carlmurg sprang toward him angrily. Lenserg seized Alla Stimney roughly by the arm.

Then there came an interruption that startled all of them, save perhaps Alla Stimney. The hall door crashed in and men spilled into the room. The door that led to the adjoining room was crashed in also, and more men entered. There was a quick rush. Carlmurg whirled angrily, was off guard for an instant, and Marpe was upon him and knocked the pistol from his hand. Lenserg found himself in the grip of two men.

Major Sinlon suddenly stood in the center of the room.

"Good!" he snapped. "Get them securely! Get those doors shut, some of you men!"

Creighton Marpe was just commencing to visualize what had happened. He saw half a dozen army officers in uniform. He saw other men that he knew were police officers and hotel employees. And then Major Sinlon was clasping him by the hand.

"Good boy, Marpe!" he snapped. "Was with Miss Stimney when you called for help so cleverly. We made our arrangements swiftly. These officers were with me, as a sort of escort for that document you are supposed to have brought me. So here we are!"

"Glad to see you, Major!" Marpe said, grinning.

"Give me that confounded thing and relieve yourself of a lot of anxiety. Miss Stimney will tell you that I am Sinlon."

"I've seen your photograph, Major. But there was a little password —"

"I'll whisper it in your ear." The major did so.

"Good enough!" Marpe said. "You want that rare document now? These men searched me, but they didn't find it."

"Want to get the thing privately?"

"That's not necessary. I never use the same hiding place twice," replied the man who changed rooms.

He sat down and removed his right shoe. At the edge of the sole, he found and touched a tiny spring. The sole came away. And there, in a hollow space not more than an eight of an inch deep, folded neatly, was the precious paper.

Marpe arose and handed it to Major Sinlon. Lenserg and Carlmurg growled oaths.

"They might have examined the heels," Marpe said. "Hollow heels are old stuff. But the sole was different. And now, if you don't mind, I am going to take Alla to lunch. She had a date with Carlmurg, but she won't be able to keep it now."

www.ingramcontent.com/pod-product-compliance
Lightning Source LLC
Chambersburg PA
CBHW030541180626
46810CB00005B/1960